KU-195-683

For my mother and father.
They did their best.
R. A.

To Hannah Butcher and her boys.
P. D.

First published in Great Britain 2021 by Walker Books Ltd
87 Vauxhall Walk, London SE11 5HJ

This edition published 2022

10 9 8 7 6 5 4 3 2 1

Text © 2020 Raymond Antrobus
Illustrations © 2020 Polly Dunbar

The right of Raymond Antrobus and Polly Dunbar to be identified
as the author and illustrator respectively of this work has been asserted
by them in accordance with the Copyright, Designs and Patents Act 1988

This book has been typeset in Archer

Printed in China

All rights reserved. No part of this book may be reproduced, transmitted or stored in
an information retrieval system in any form or by any means, graphic, electronic or mechanical,
including photocopying, taping and recording, without prior written permission from the publisher.

British Library Cataloguing in Publication Data:
a catalogue record for this book is available from the British Library

ISBN 978-1-4063-9462-7

www.walker.co.uk

Amnesty endorses this book because
every child has the right to learn and play.

3 0 JUL

29 OCT

2

If not require
person, by po
To renew, eith

24 HO

This Walker book belongs to:

_____

_____

_____

STAFFORDSHIRE LIBRARIES

3 8014 09548 191 4

Can Bears Ski?

Raymond Antrobus

illustrated by
Polly Dunbar

WALKER BOOKS
AND SUBSIDIARIES
LONDON · BOSTON · SYDNEY · AUCKLAND

Dad Bear has a hard time waking me up in the morning.

"ONE."
The radiator shakes.

"TWO."
The bed rumbles like a large empty tummy.

"THREE."
The windows by the bed tremble.

"FOUR."
Dad Bear takes one heavy step forward.

The ceiling cracks.

"FIVE..."

My eyes snap awake.

I explode out of bed!

My feet hit the ground.

"I'M UP! I'M UP!"

I put on sky-blue socks,

and my orange trousers and yellow jumper.

I like my colours LOUD!

It's been snowing!

Everything feels still –
no rumbling,
no trembling.
It's like everything
is breathing quietly.

Then I feel Dad's voice.

"ONE."
Banisters shake.

"TWO."
Pictures wobble.

"THREE."
Stairs flinch.

"I'm coming. I'm coming!" I say.

I gobble-gobble breakfast.
Dad Bear has the TV on.
I can see a man in a blue bodysuit
skiing fast down a slope.

Dad Bear is saying something to me.

I think he says, **"Can bears ski?"**

I shrug.
I'm not sure I heard him right.

I eat the last of my porridge.
Time for school.

Dad Bear talks a lot
on our way to school.
I hear the
crunch
crunch
crunch
of the snow.

Dad Bear stops and looks directly at me.
"Your friend was saying hello.
Why did you ignore him?"
"I didn't." *I didn't.*

Then Dad Bear asks again, **"CAN BEARS SKI?"**

Is that really what he's asking me?

Teacher Bear approaches Dad Bear.
I can only hear little pieces
of what they are saying.

"... have to sit ...

front of class..."

Teacher Bear stamps on the ground.
I feel the ground shake, so I look up.

He is saying something to me,
but I can't quite work it out.
I wonder if it's **"Can bears ski?"**

David Bear sits next to me at lunch. He is talking a lot.
Suddenly laughter bursts out everywhere.
I don't know what everyone is laughing at.

He asks me a question.
"Can bears ski?"

I don't know.

Shhhhhhhh.

One day Dad Bear picks me up early.
We are going to meet someone
with a name I can't say.

She writes her name like this:
au-di-ol-o-gist.
It's a really hard word to say.

She puts headphones on my head.
She wants me to put a block on
the table every time I hear a sound.

Then she shows us something
called an **au-dio-gram.**

It's also a hard word to say.

On the **au-dio-gram**
my results are the shape
of a ski slope.

I imagine myself skiing down it.

The au-di-ol-o-gist asks,

"CAN BEARS SKI?"

After a week and
a few more
tests ...

I start hearing therapy and
lip-reading classes, too!

The au-di-ol-o-gist gives me plastic ears called hearing aids.

They feel uncomfortable at first. Everything sounds like robots.

The au-di-ol-o-gist asks, "C

AN YOU HEAR ME?"

Whoa... *Is life this loud?!*

Sometimes I get tired and sound stops making sense, no matter how loud it is.

Sometimes I take my hearing aids out and lose them. Guess I'm not used to them yet.

Can bears ski?

I still don't know
how to answer that question.

Dad Bear reads a story aloud.
He looks directly at me.
I can see his whole face
and he speaks clearly.

I can feel his big voice and
see the words on the page,
so I follow Dad Bear's finger.

There is a big picture
of the moon.

I know what the moon is saying
because I can see its whole face
and the moon is speaking clearly.

"Can you hear me?"
says the moon.

I say,
"Bears CAN ski!"

Learn the British Sign Language alphabet with

Can Bears Ski?

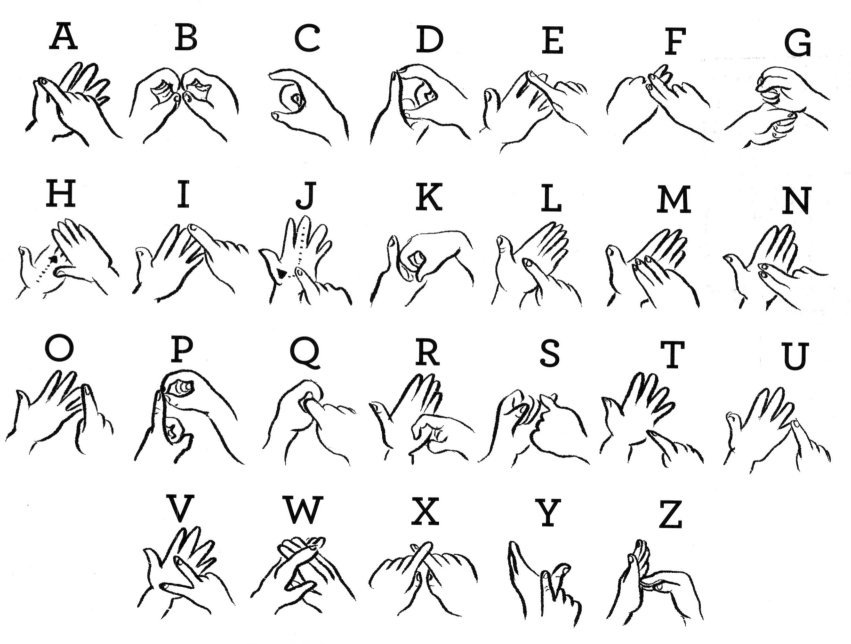

This alphabet is for those who are right-handed;
for left-handed instructions visit www.british-sign.co.uk